THIS WALKER BOOK BELONGS TO:

_____

_____

_____ ' 2017

WALKER BOOKS is the world's leading independent publisher of children's books. Working with the best authors and illustrators we create books for all ages, from babies to teenagers – books your child will grow up with and always remember. So…

FOR THE BEST CHILDREN'S BOOKS, LOOK FOR THE BEAR

Making a friend.

a place to hide

a pony ride

let's pretend

a happy end and . . .

What we all like is...

a Christmas tree

watching TV

fleas

peas

bees

aches

snakes

breaks

bumps

lumps

dumps

rats

gnats

bats

I don't like...

playing the fool   a swimming pool   nursery school

I love...

ice-cream

a funny dream

my thermos flask

my monster mask

What I like is...

playing with my mother

and my new baby brother

I like…

thunder and lightning

I hate…

being a pair

people who stare

having to share

Sometimes
we don't like…

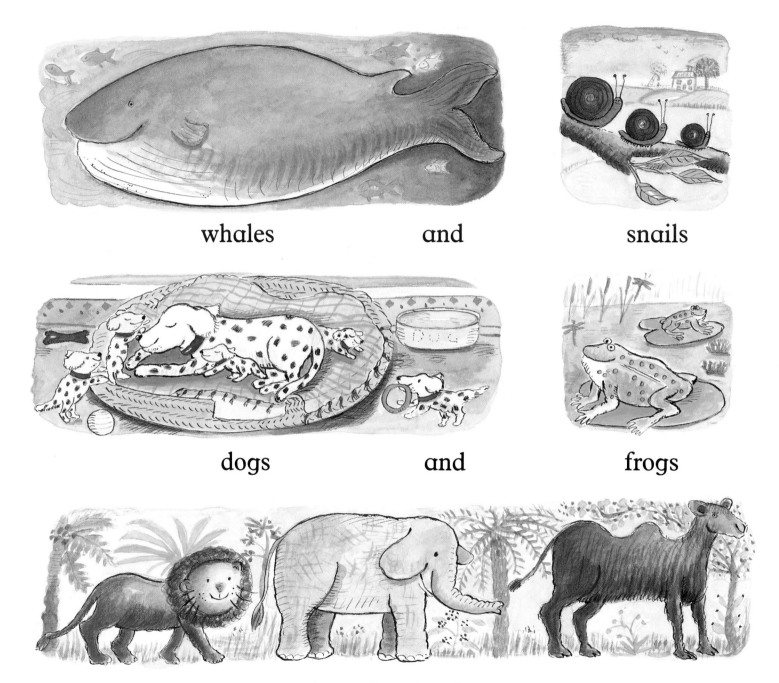

whales   and   snails

dogs   and   frogs

lots of animals

I love...

getting lost

I don't like...

jumping about

having a shout

going out

What we like is...

time to play

a holiday

toys

(some) boys

waking early

hair all curly

What I like is...

What I Like

Catherine and Laurence Anholt

WALKER BOOKS
AND SUBSIDIARIES
LONDON • BOSTON • SYDNEY • AUCKLAND

For Maria and Joe

First published 1991 by Walker Books Ltd
87 Vauxhall Walk, London SE11 5HJ

This edition published 2006

4 6 8 10 9 7 5 3

© 1991, 2006 Catherine and Laurence Anholt

The right of Laurence and Catherine Anholt to be identified as
author and illustrator respectively of this work has been asserted by them
in accordance with the Copyright, Designs and Patents Act 1988

This book has been typeset in Plantin Educational

Printed in China

British Library Cataloguing in Publication Data:
a catalogue record for this book is available from the British Library.

ISBN 978-1-4063-0345-2

www.walkerbooks.co.uk